Need a Trim, Jim

For the lady who
gave me the idea – K.U.

For Joe Daniels
with love from MC

1 3 5 7 9 10 8 6 4 2
Text copyright © Kaye Umansky, 1999
Illustrations copyright © Margaret Chamberlain, 1999
Kaye Umansky & Margaret Chamberlain have asserted their right under the Copyright, Designs and Patents Act,
1988, to be identified as the author and illustrator of this work. First published in the United Kingdom 1999
by The Bodley Head Children's Books, Random House, 20 Vauxhall Bridge Road, London SW1V 2SA
Random House Australia (Pty) Limited, 20 Alfred Street, Milsons Point, Sydney, New South Wales 2061, Australia
Random House New Zealand Limited, 18 Poland Road, Glenfield, Auckland 10, New Zealand
Random House South Africa (Pty) Limited, Endulini, 5A Jubilee Road, Parktown 2193, South Africa
Random House UK Limited Reg. No. 954009 A CIP catalogue record for this book is available from the British Library
ISBN 0 370 32328 9   Printed in Hong Kong

Need A Trim, Jim

Kaye Umansky &
Margaret Chamberlain

THE BODLEY HEAD
LONDON

Look at Jim! He needs a trim.
His hair's so long, he cannot see.

He falls down stairs,

bumps into chairs

and has such trouble
with his tea.

He misses balls,

walks into walls

and you should see
him in the rain!

Come on, Jim, you need a trim.
It's time we saw your eyes again.

Hello, Clare! I *love* your hair!
You've had it cut, it's really cute.

There goes Pete, now, his is neat.
And goes so nicely with his suit.

Here comes Shirley, blonde and curly
(Twenty brush strokes every day!)
Gail has got a pony tail.
She says it keeps the flies away.

Dot has got an awful lot.
She wears it in a tidy plait.

Mike has spikes and Dave has waves
And George has gel to keep his flat.

What a lot of lovely hair styles
We've seen in the park today.

Looking forward to your trim, Jim?
What's that Jim? What did you say?

Does it hurt to have your hair cut?
Don't be silly. Not at all.

They simply take a pair of scissors...
Jim! Come back! Slow down, you'll fall!

Jim's escaping! Stop him, someone!
Ouch! He's run into a tree.

Now he's fallen in a puddle.

Now he's tripped and hurt his knee.

Poor old Jim. Cheer up. Don't cry.
You just can't see through all that hair.

Let's ask someone for a plaster.
There's a shop, just over there.

There, that's better. Feel more cheerful?
Got a tissue? Dry your face.

See the goldfish? Want a biscuit?
Isn't this a jolly place?

Let's make faces in the mirror.
Let's just pop you in the seat...

Snip, snip, snip! And there's your trim, Jim!
Honest, Jim. You look real sweet.